For Dorothy,

with lots of love from Gumble. x

V. F.

For Patsy, Amelia, Cora, Catnip,

and Dexter the dog.

With lots of thanks to Reception class,

Great Tew School.

S. H.

First U.S. edition 2010

Library of Congress Cataloging-in-Publication Data

French, Vivian.
Polly's pink pajamas / Vivian French ; illustrated by Sue Heap. — 1st U.S. ed.
p.   cm.
Summary: Polly loves her pink pajamas so much that she wears them day and night, but when Fred invites
her to a party, she visits all of her friends to borrow the special clothes she thinks she will need.
ISBN 978-0-7636-4807-7
[1. Clothing and dress — Fiction. 2. Pajamas — Fiction. 3. Humorous stories.]
I. Heap, Sue, ill. II. Title.
PZ7.F88917Pol 2010
[E] — dc22   2009032503

10 11 12 13 14 15 16 CCP 10 9 8 7 6 5 4 3 2 1

Printed in Shenzhen, Guangdong, China

This book was typeset in Carnation.
The illustrations were done in crayon and acrylic paint.

Candlewick Press
99 Dover Street
Somerville, Massachusetts 02144

visit us at www.candlewick.com

CANDLEWICK PRESS

Polly's Pink Pajamas

Vivian French   Sue Heap

Polly loved her pink pajamas.

♥ ♥ ♥ ♥ ♥ ♥

What did she wear
when she went
to bed?

♥ ♥ ♥

PINK PAJAMAS!

What did she wear
when she got up?

♥ ♥ ♥

PINK PAJAMAS!

What did she wear
when she ate her
breakfast?

♥ ♥ ♥

PINK PAJAMAS!

What did Polly wear ALL DAY LONG?

PINK PAJAMAS!

Then, one Monday morning,
RAT-A-TAT-TAT!

Polly ran to open
the front door.

"Hello, Polly!" said Fred.
"Will you come to my party?"
"Yes please," said Polly. "I LOVE parties!"
"Good!" said Fred. "Come over to my house at five o'clock."

And off he ran.

"Oh," said Polly.
"What shall I wear?

I need
a DRESS, a SWEATER,
SOCKS, and SHOES.
♥ ♥ ♥

I know! I'll go and see Mia."

Polly ran to Mia's house.

● ○ ● ♥ ● ○ ●

"Hello, Mia, I need a dress!"

"You can have my red polka-dot dress,"
said Mia.

"Thank you,"
said Polly, and she
put on the dress.

"And now I'll go and see Jo."

Polly hurried to Jo's house.

"Jo! Jo! I need a sweater!"

"You can have my green checkered sweater," said Jo.

"Thank you,"
said Polly, and she
put on the sweater.

"And now I'll go and see Harry."

Polly rushed to Harry's house.

"Hello, Harry, I need some socks!"

"You can borrow my striped socks," said Harry.

"Thank you,"
said Polly,
and she pulled on the socks.

♥ ♥ ♥

"One last thing," Polly told herself.
"I'll go and see Claire."

Polly rushed to Claire's house.

"Claire! Claire! I need some shoes!"
"You can have my blue
shiny shoes," said Claire.

"Thank you,"
said Polly, and she
put on the shoes.

"Thank you very much INDEED!"

Polly went home.

♥ ♥ ♥ ♥ ♥

"Now I'm ready for the party!" she said.

She went to look in the mirror.

She stared and she stared

and she stared.

The red polka-dot dress
was MUCH too SHORT.

The green checkered sweater
was MUCH too SMALL.

The striped socks
were MUCH too LONG.

And the blue shiny shoes
were MUCH too BIG.

♥ ♥ ♥ ♥ ♥

"Oh, NO!" said Polly.

And she cried and she cried
and she cried.

Until . . .

Ting-a-ling! Ting-a-ling!
The phone rang.

♥ ♥ ♥

Polly answered it.

♥ ♥ ♥

Polly," said Fred. "Why aren't you at my party?"

Oh, Fred!" sobbed Polly. "I can't come to your party!

I haven't got any party clothes!"

But, Polly," said Fred, "it's not a party-clothes party.

It's a SPECIAL party.

We're going to have PIZZA.

We're going to have HOT CHOCOLATE.

Dad's reading us

BEDTIME

STORIES. . . .

It's a PAJAMA party!"

"HURRAH!" shouted Polly.

"Hurrah, hurrah,
HURRAH!

I'll be there
in just a minute!"

And Polly took off

the blue shiny shoes,

the striped socks,

the green checkered sweater,

and the red polka-dot dress.

And what do you think
Polly wore to Fred's party?

PINK PAJAMAS!